Blanket & Bear, a Remarkable Pair

L. J. R. KELLY

illustrated by
YOKO TANAKA

G. P. PUTNAM'S SONS • AN IMPRINT OF PENGUIN GROUP (USA) INC.

For Maureen, who tamed the fires of our childhood
and loved us all equally (but Clover most).
—L. J. R. K.

For my mother, P.R.
—Y. T.

G. P. PUTNAM'S SONS
A division of Penguin Young Readers Group.
Published by The Penguin Group.
Penguin Group (USA) Inc., 375 Hudson Street, New York, NY 10014, U.S.A.
Penguin Group (Canada), 90 Eglinton Avenue East, Suite 700, Toronto, Ontario M4P 2Y3, Canada
(a division of Pearson Penguin Canada Inc.).
Penguin Books Ltd, 80 Strand, London WC2R 0RL, England.
Penguin Ireland, 25 St. Stephen's Green, Dublin 2, Ireland (a division of Penguin Books Ltd).
Penguin Group (Australia), 707 Collins Street, Melbourne, Victoria 3008, Australia
(a division of Pearson Australia Group Pty Ltd).
Penguin Books India Pvt Ltd, 11 Community Centre, Panchsheel Park, New Delhi—110 017, India.
Penguin Group (NZ), 67 Apollo Drive, Rosedale, Auckland 0632, New Zealand
(a division of Pearson New Zealand Ltd).
Penguin Books South Africa, Rosebank Office Park, 181 Jan Smuts Avenue, Parktown North 2193, South Africa.
Penguin China, B7 Jiaming Center, 27 East Third Ring Road North, Chaoyang District, Beijing 100020, China.
Penguin Books Ltd, Registered Offices: 80 Strand, London WC2R 0RL, England.

Published simultaneously in Canada. Manufactured in China by South China Printing Co. Ltd.
Text set in Plantin Infant. The art was done in acrylic on illustration board.

Library of Congress Cataloging-in-Publication Data
Kelly, L.J.R. Blanket and bear, a remarkable pair / by L.J.R. Kelly ; illustrated by Yoko Tanaka.
p. cm. Summary: When a boy loses his beloved blanket and bear, they travel a great distance to make
their way back to him. [1. Stories in rhyme. 2. Lost and found possessions—Fiction. 3. Blankets—Fiction.
4. Teddy bears—Fiction.] I. Tanaka, Yoko, ill. II. Title. PZ8.3.K3329Bl 2013 [E]—dc23 2012009638
ISBN 978-0-399-25681-3
1 3 5 7 9 10 8 6 4 2

Here comes a story
of a blanket and bear
owned by a boy
who left them somewhere.

The boy met the bear
on the day he was born.
And with the blanket to cuddle,
he was cozy and warm.

The blanket was tattered
by the boy's loving care.

And wherever he went,
so went the bear.

One day he was traveling
with them both by his side.

But then they were gone—

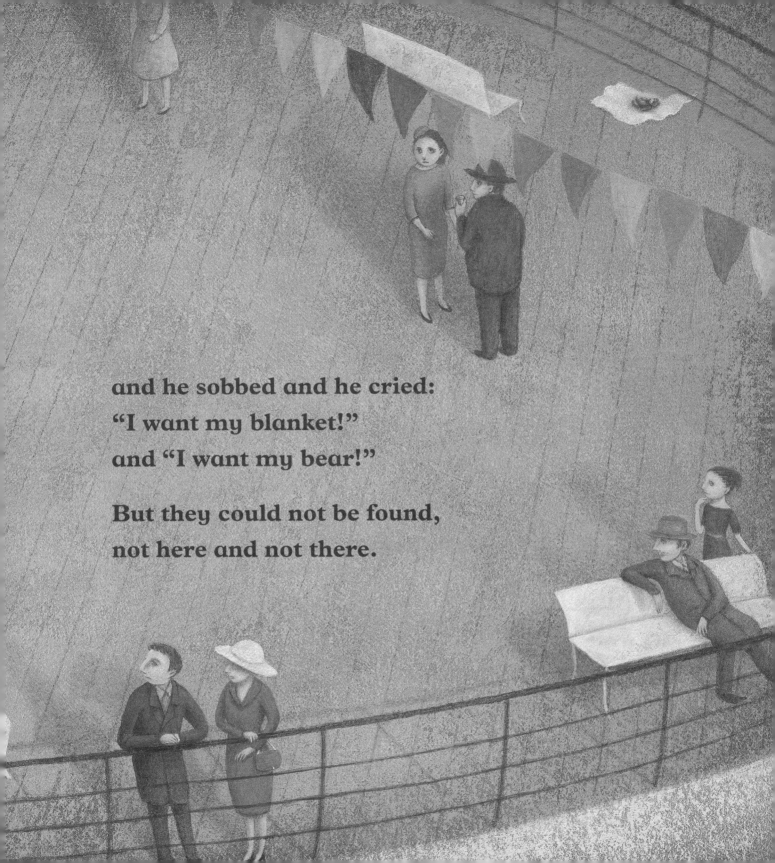

and he sobbed and he cried:
"I want my blanket!"
and "I want my bear!"

But they could not be found,
not here and not there.

Over the oceans
and across distant lands,

they sailed and they flew
to get back in his hands.

They arrived at an island
of lost blankets and bears,
living in retirement,
without worries or cares.

"Stay," said the King.
"Make this your new home.
The boy will replace you—
he won't be alone."

"They say you are lost,
but this is where you belong."
The king begged them to stay,
but they traveled on.

Forward they went,
through fields and through streams,

searching for the boy
they saw in their dreams.

At long last they found him—
so grown-up! so tall!—
racing straight past them
to dive for a ball.

Their eyes filled with tears,
for they saw it was true—

they were no longer needed.
Their time was now through.

So back they went to the island
of lost blankets and bears,
joining the others
without worries or cares.

No longer owned,
free to do as they wish:
to dance and tell stories,
to swim and to fish.

Now think for a minute
of the toys you once knew.
Are they now on that island,
telling stories of you?